Annie and Snowball and the Wintry Freeze

The Eighth Book of Their Adventures

Cynthia Rylant

Illustrated by Suçie Stevenson

READY-TO-READ

SIMON SPOTLIGHT

New York   London   Toronto   Sydney

For Liza Voges
—S. S.

SIMON SPOTLIGHT
An imprint of Simon & Schuster Children's Publishing Division
1230 Avenue of the Americas, New York, New York 10020
Text copyright © 2010 by Cynthia Rylant
Illustrations copyright © 2010 by Suçie Stevenson
All rights reserved, including the right of reproduction
in whole or in part in any form.
SIMON SPOTLIGHT, READY-TO-READ, and colophon
are registered trademarks of Simon & Schuster, Inc.
For information about special discounts for bulk purchases, please contact
Simon & Schuster Special Sales at 1-866-506-1949 or business@simonandschuster.com.
Designed by Tom Daly
The text of this book was set in Goudy.
The illustrations for this book were rendered in pen-and-ink and watercolor.
Manufactured in the United States of America 0911 LAK
First Simon Spotlight paperback edition October 2011
2 4 6 8 10 9 7 5 3 1
The Library of Congress has cataloged the hardcover edition as follows:
Rylant, Cynthia.
Annie and Snowball and the wintry freeze / Cynthia Rylant;
illustrated by Suçie Stevenson.
p. cm. — (Ready-to-read)
Summary: Annie and her cousin Henry, along with Henry's dog Mudge and
Annie's rabbit Snowball, enjoy a sparkling, wintry ice storm.
[1. Ice storms—Fiction. 2. Winter—Fiction. 3. Cousins—Fiction. 4. Pets—Fiction.]
I. Stevenson, Suçie, ill. II. Title.
PZ7.R982Anw 2010
[E]—dc22
2009032066
ISBN 978-1-4169-7206-8 (pbk)
ISBN 978-1-4169-7205-1 (hc)
ISBN 978-1-4169-8254-8 (eBook)

Contents

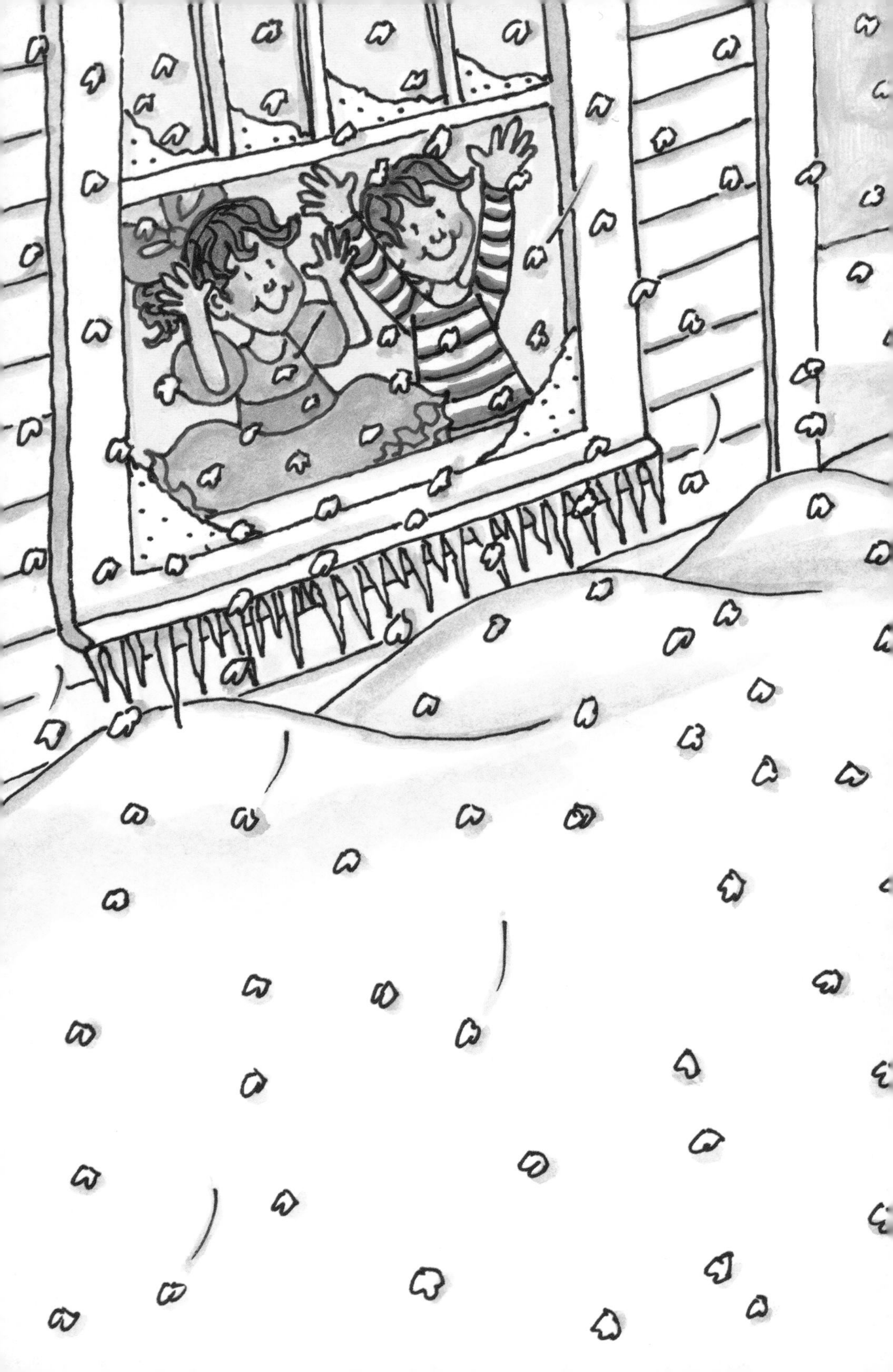

Winter!

It was winter, and Annie and
her cousin Henry were very happy.
They both loved winter.

Henry loved the snow forts
and the snowmen.

Annie loved the muffs:
earmuffs and hand muffs, all in pink!
Plus her pink polka-dot boots!

Annie waited through spring
and summer and fall for the time
to wear her muffs and boots.
Winter was here!

Annie and Henry were not the only
ones who loved winter.
Henry's big dog, Mudge, and Annie's
bunny, Snowball, also loved winter.

Mudge loved it because snow
was one of his favorite foods.

Snowball loved it because she
had a cozy box by the fireplace.
And also because she was a *Snow*ball!
Winter was wonderful.

Bundle!

One morning Annie's dad woke her
and told her there would be
no school that day.

13

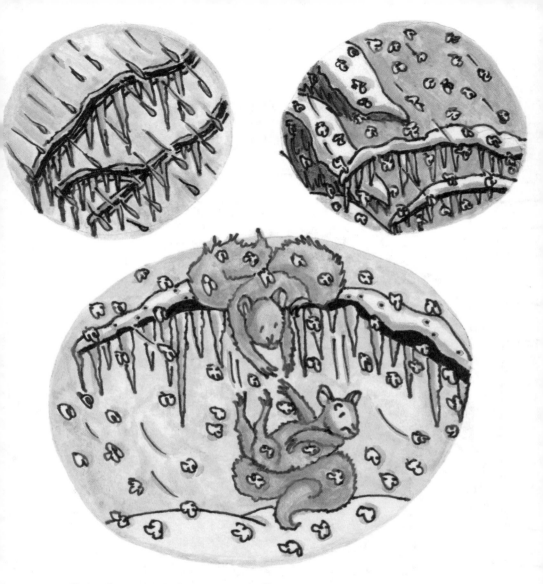

"A freeze is coming,"
said her dad.
"Icy rain, icy snow,
icy everything," he said.
"Wow," said Annie.

15

She called Henry right away.

He was already looking for his ice skates.

"Do you have ice skates?"
he asked Annie.
"No," said Annie. "No skates."

"That's okay," said Henry.
"We'll figure something out.
Just bundle up.
It's freezing out there!"

Annie bundled up.

She bundled so well that her dad
said she looked like a
big pink marshmallow.
Annie just smiled.

19

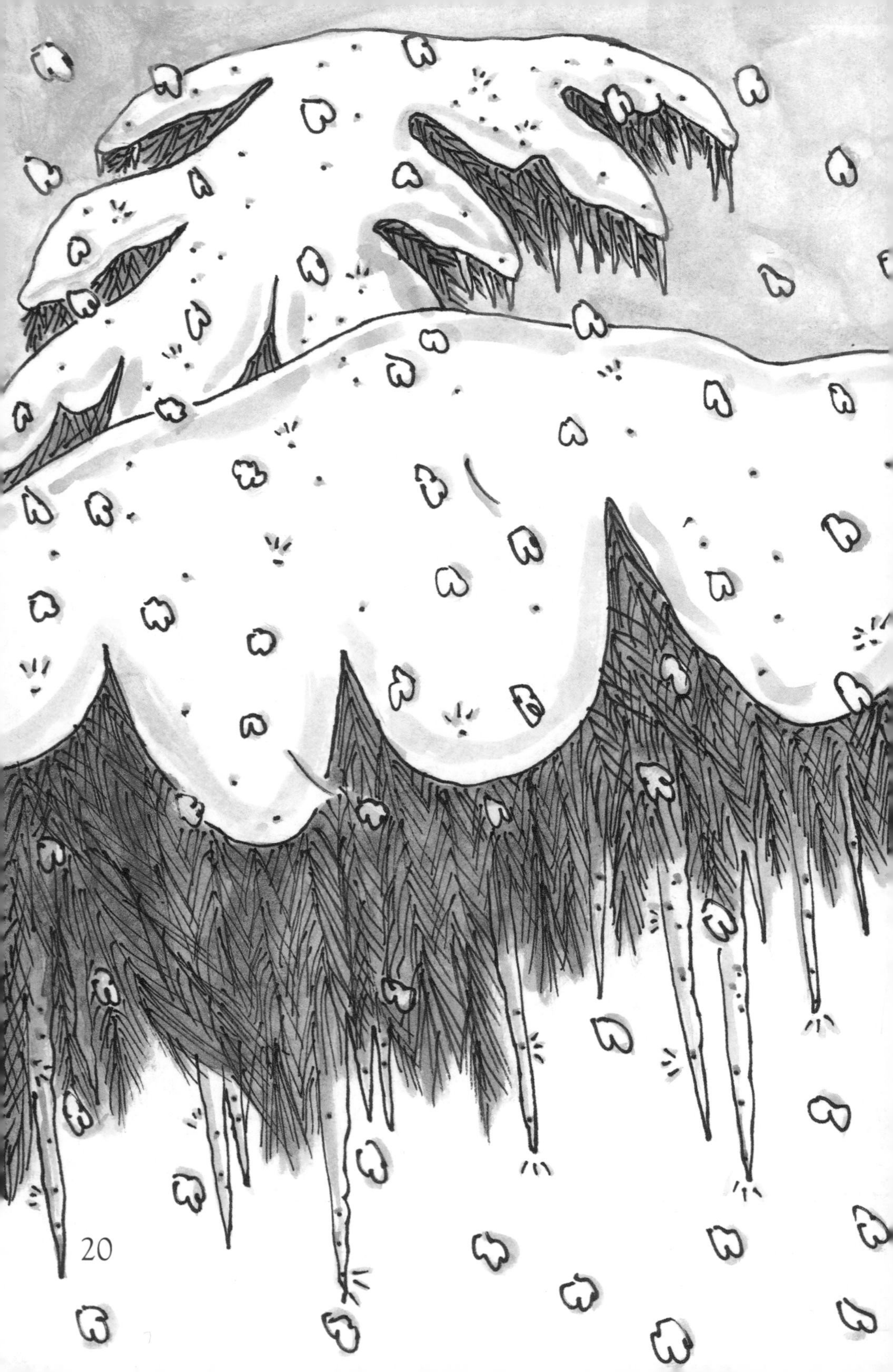

Icy Everything

The icy rain came first.
Then it turned to icy snow.
Then it seemed the whole world
was made of ice.

Annie and Henry and Mudge explored.
Mudge was wearing a
doggy coat and doggy boots.

Henry was wearing ice skates
and a snowsuit.

And Annie was wearing every pink
warm thing she could find
from her closet.
She was also holding on to Mudge
for dear life.

It was *very* slippery on the icy ground!
Henry could skate.
But Annie could only slide.
She held on to Mudge and slid
all over the place.

25

She slid in the yard.

She slid on the sidewalk.

She slid right up to the window
where Snowball was sitting.
Snowball had stayed inside
at Henry's house.
It was too cold for little bunnies
to play outside.

Mudge looked at Snowball
and wagged.
Henry looked at Snowball
and waved.

Annie blew Snowball a kiss.
Snowball looked happy to be
warm and cozy.

Annie was happy to be
cold and icy.
The world covered in ice
was *beautiful*, and she
loved it.

She and Henry and Mudge
explored every sparkling thing.

31

Warmed Up

When it was time to get warm,
Annie went into Henry's house.
Henry's dad had been filling the
bird and squirrel feeders.
He was cold too.
So he warmed up some apple cider
and some cinnamon buns.
"*Yum*," said Annie.

33

They peeled off their icy mittens
and icy hats and icy boots.

Henry's dad helped Mudge
peel off his icy things.

Then Annie and Henry and Mudge
sat in front of the fire
and warmed every finger
and toe and paw.

When Annie was all warmed up,
she found Snowball.
Annie offered Snowball a bit of
her cinnamon bun.

Then they both snuggled into Mudge
by the fire.

Outside, the world sparkled.

Inside, Annie sparkled.

She just loved a wintry freeze!